I just ate my friend

I just ate my friend

HEIDI MCKINNON

Simon & Schuster Books for Young Readers
New York London Toronto Sydney New Delhi

I just ate my friend.

He was a good friend,
but now he's gone.

Hello! Would you be my friend?

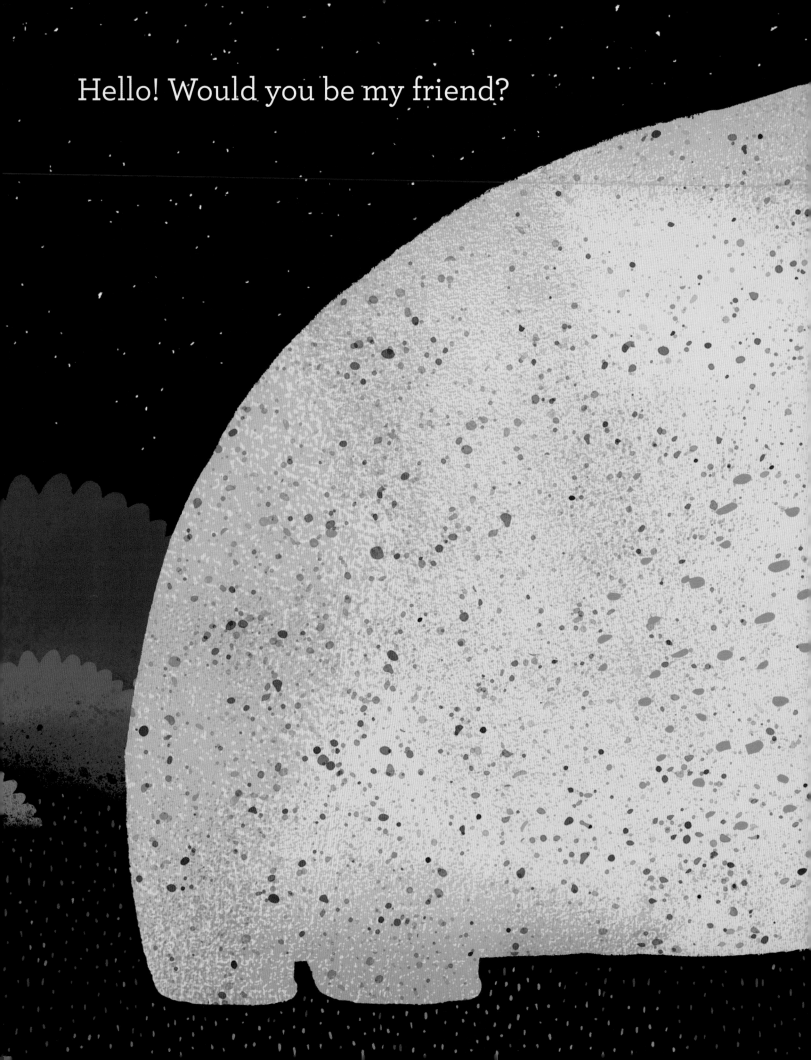

No, you are too big.

Hello! Would you be my friend?

No, you are too small.

Hello! Would you be my friend?

No, you are too scary.

Hello! Would you be my friend?

No, you are too slow.

Hello! Would you be my friend?

No.

Hello! Would you be my . . .

Never mind.

Good-bye.

What if I never find another friend?

What if I ate my only friend?

Hello! I will be your friend.

I just ate my friend.

FOR
Seamus and Ava

A huge thanks to:
Sally Rippin, Susannah Chambers, Cam at dirtypuppet.com,
and my incredible dad, Sandy McKinnon.

SIMON & SCHUSTER BOOKS FOR YOUNG READERS
An imprint of Simon & Schuster Children's Publishing Division
1230 Avenue of the Americas, New York, New York 10020
Copyright © 2017 by Heidi McKinnon
First published in Australia in 2017 by Allen & Unwin
First US edition 2018
All rights reserved, including the right of reproduction in whole or in part in any form.
SIMON & SCHUSTER BOOKS FOR YOUNG READERS is a trademark of Simon & Schuster, Inc.
For information about special discounts for bulk purchases, please contact Simon & Schuster
Special Sales at 1-866-506-1949 or business@simonandschuster.com.
The Simon & Schuster Speakers Bureau can bring authors to your live event. For more information or to book an event,
contact the Simon & Schuster Speakers Bureau at 1-866-248-3049 or visit our website at www.simonspeakers.com.
Also available in a Simon & Schuster Books for Young Readers hardcover edition
The text for this book was set in Archer.
The illustrations for this book were rendered in ink and brush, then Photoshop.
Manufactured in China
0919 SCP
First Simon & Schuster Books for Young Readers paperback edition December 2019
2 4 6 8 10 9 7 5 3 1
The Library of Congress has cataloged the hardcover edition as follows:
Names: McKinnon, Heidi, author.
Title: I just ate my friend / Heidi McKinnon.
Description: First edition. | New York : Simon & Schuster Books for Young Readers, [2018] | "First published in Australia in 2017
by Allen & Unwin"—Title page verso. | Summary: Having eaten his only friend, a monster seeks a new
companion but each creature he meets has a good reason not to serve as a replacement.
Identifiers: LCCN 2017029055| ISBN 9781534410329 (hardcover) |
ISBN 9781534466685 (paperback) | ISBN 9781534410336 (eBook)
Subjects: | CYAC: Friendship—Fiction. | Monsters—Fiction. | Behavior—Fiction. | Humorous stories.
Classification: LCC PZ7.1.M43547 Iaf 2018 | DDC [E]—dc23
LC record available at https://lccn.loc.gov/2017029055